Mess Monsters
at Christmas

Beth Shoshan

Illustrated by
Piers Harper

Albury Books

One day Mummy said
That her plans were a mess,
"It's Christmas tomorrow,
I'm feeling the stress!"

I said,

"Mummy, calm down,
It's better that way,
Whenever you're worried
Those 'friends' come and play."

So, as you and I know,
Just under the tree,
Is a big gang of monsters
Who are waiting for me...

First **a leg,**

then an arm,

Then a great **tangled** mess.

Just what comes from what bit
Is anyone's guess!

Those **te_{rr}ible** monsters **burst** in through the door,

Munching and slurping
And howling for more...

The presents, unopened,

Were **flung** through the air,

As bangles and baubles

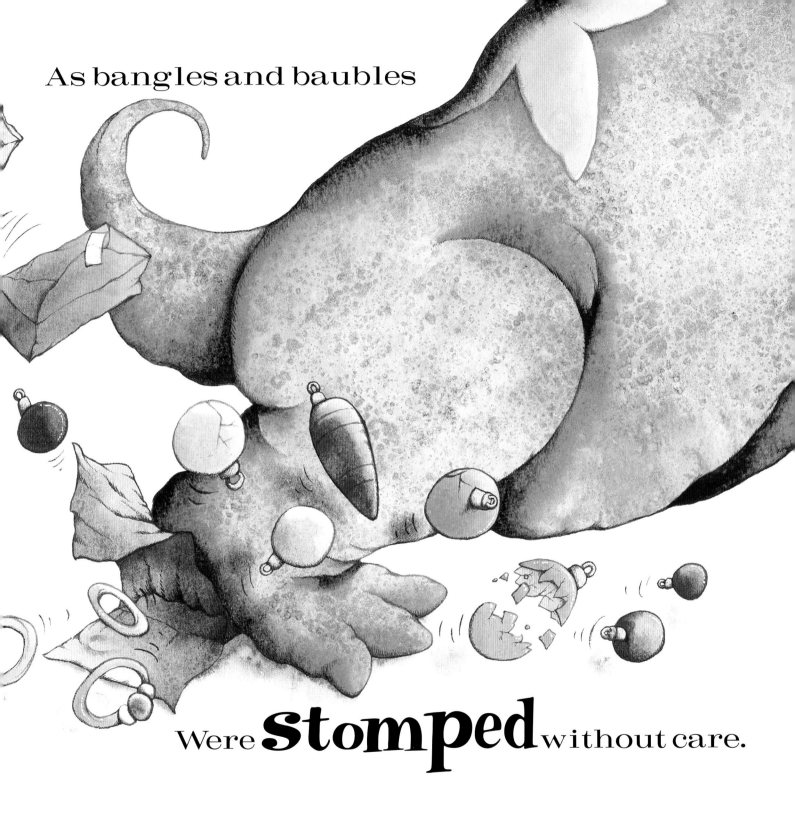

Were **stomped** without care.

The angels looked worried,
But Teddy was
STRONG!

Then they **thrashed** him

mashed and him

Although it was wrong.

They **swung** from the tinsel,
Put snow everywhere.

Then **flattened** the snowman, Demolished a chair.

I'd seen what I needed,
Then shouted,

Oi!

Stop!

And reminded the
monsters
That mess has to stop.

I spoke about Christmas
And what we all need,
About giving and helping
And doing good deeds.

So they looked at each other

And, I think, understood

About all of the nice things,

And how to do good.

They packed all the presents
(Then added some more)
They made me a Snowman...

...Put stars on the door.

They hung all the tinsel
And worked through the
night,

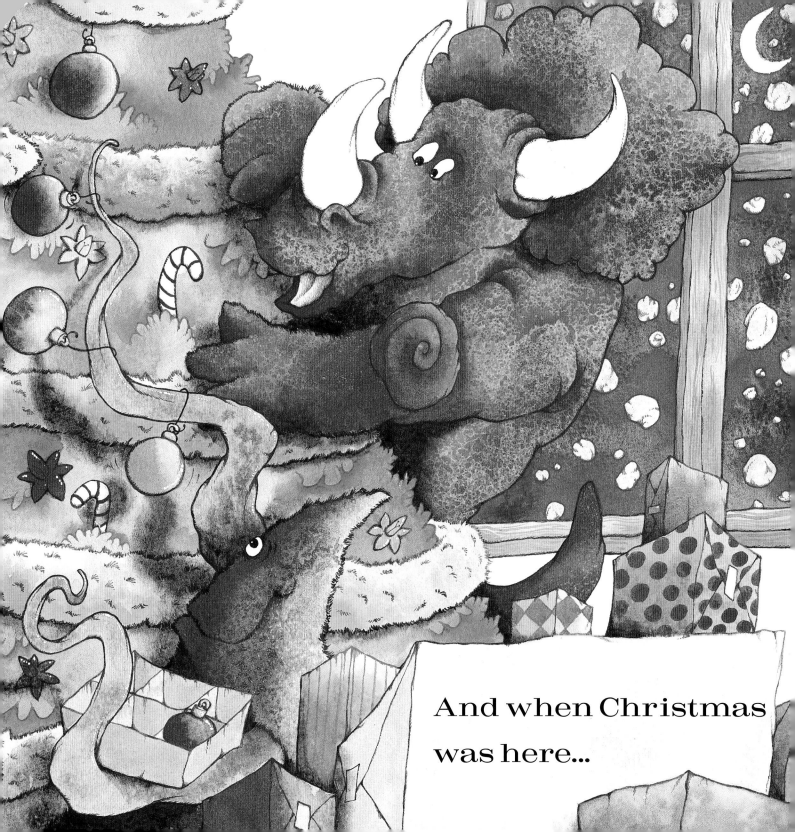

And when Christmas
was here...

...what a fabulous sight!

Now it's Christmas today
And a time to reflect;
You just won't feel calm
If your house **is a** Wreck!

For
Rupert
B.S.

For
Dan, Nick and Sadie
P.H.

First published in 2006
This edition published by Albury Books in 2014
Albury Court, Albury, Thame,
Oxfordshire, OX9 2LP, United Kingdom

Text Beth Shoshan, 2006
Illustrations © Piers Harper, 2006

A CIP catalogue record for this book
is available from the British Library

Printed in China

ISBN 978-1-909958-21-0

For orders: Kuperard Publishers & Distributors
+44 (0) 208 4462440